DON'T LEAVE AN ELEPHANT
TO GO AND CHASE A BIRD

RETOLD BY **JAMES BERRY**

ILLUSTRATED BY **ANN GRIFALCONI**

SIMON & SCHUSTER BOOKS FOR YOUNG READERS

Simon & Schuster Books for Young Readers
An imprint of Simon & Schuster Children's Publishing Division
1230 Avenue of the Americas
New York, NY 10020
Text copyright © 1996 by James Berry
Illustrations copyright © 1996 by Ann Grifalconi
SIMON & SCHUSTER BOOKS FOR YOUNG READERS is a trademark of Simon & Schuster.

Book design by Anahid Hamparian
The text of this book is set in 13 point Hiroshige medium.
The illustrations were done in poster colors.
Manufactured in the United States of America
10 9 8 7 6 5 4 3 2 1

Library of Congress Cataloging-in-Publication Data
Berry, James.
Don't leave an elephant to go and chase a bird / by James Berry ;
illustrated by Ann Grifalconi
p.   cm.
Summary: Anancy Spiderman trades various items with the people he encounters, until he
himself is distracted by a bird and ends up empty-handed.
ISBN 0-689-80464-4
[1. Anansi (Legendary character) 2. Folklore—Ghana.]
I. Grifalconi, Ann, ill. II. Title.
PZ8.1.B4187Do   1996
398.2'096670452544—dc20
[E]   94-24317

AUTHOR'S NOTE

Don't Leave an Elephant to Go and Chase a Bird *is a retelling based on a story originally collected in Ghana in the 1920s.*

*Collected and translated by anthropologist Capt. R. S. Rattray, the original story was published in 1930 by Oxford University Press in the book **Akan-Ashanti Folk-Tales**.*

The spider hero Anancy and his stories came from Africa and settled in the Caribbean with us over the centuries. But my retelling here does not at all change either the structure, substance, or meaning of this fresh story. My understanding of the Jamaican traditional telling of Anancy stories merely helped me to dress it up.

The original story surely had its untouchable qualities. It had its own dynamic material and structure maintaining its individuality. It was also recorded in one long paragraph.

The essence of the story stays intact. I tried to merely transfer the story to a new readership and audience with a fresh language sound and energy through my Caribbean speech rhythms, unnoticeably. Its difference now is in the language that conveys it and how its parts are linked, emphasized, and highlighted for the printed page.

In Jamaican traditional stories, to trick someone, Anancy comes disguising his intentions in sugary mannerisms of speech. He will have awful affectations of innocence and humility. Yet only little suggestions of that cunning are obvious in this retelling. An example is in the first paragraph of the story:

He said "Skygod, a *good good* morning to you!"

A Jamaican audience would know Anancy to be down on his knees, saying, "Mr. Skygod, oh an ever ever good good morning to you, sir!"

Lastly, in the story a child is shared. I should explain that sharing a child was not unusual in Ghana or in my birthplace, Jamaica, West Indies, where I grew up.

Sometimes a child would be shared with childless relatives, or by special arrangements with a better educated or a wealthy family, or simply with a home that offered special opportunities. The child would keep in touch with her or his parental home. Usually for a child, it was a welcome opportunity to go and live in a smaller, better-off family in place of his or her own overcrowded one. And that child might well become the envy of other brothers and sisters.

The sharing of a child comes easily and naturally into this story. That is so because culture and custom provide their own characters and situations. Our folktale merely comes from a way of life, with its realities, myths, and images.

—JAMES BERRY

ARTIST'S NOTE

In illustrating this story, the feeling I wanted to get was that of Africans visualizing their own folktale. Having been to western Africa, I had seen their great gift for carving and decorating surfaces, so I based the style of the figures upon the popular sturdy African wood sculptures and carvings, and the background designs directly upon patterns of pure African origin (African Designs by Goeffrey Williams, copyright © 1971, Dover). The ever-popular Anancy Spiderman character was based upon a mythical figure drawn by an African (African Folktales by Roger D. Abrams, copyright © 1983, Pantheon).

—ANN GRIFALCONI

One morning Anancy Spiderman woke up. Anancy Spiderman had no idea what he was going to do today. But he knew something would happen if he started moving. He left his house and started walking along the road. Suddenly, he felt an urge and said to himself "Ugh, ugh! Something is happening!" He knew he should say good morning to Skygod.

Anancy sat down at the roadside. He said "Skygod, a *good good* morning to you!" He waited. No answer came from Skygod. "That's all right with me," he said to himself. "I'll just wait!" And he was all set to wait. All prepared to wait as long as ever. With no warning, *quick quick,* he found a corncob in his hand. Anancy smiled, knowing it was from Skygod. But he became full of thinking. Anancy Spiderman didn't know what to do with the corn-cob. He listened *hard hard* to himself. And then he knew what to do.

Anancy got up and started walking again, this time carrying the corncob in his hand.
Anancy Spiderman came to a stream. Women were there washing, beating clothes
on big rocks. "Good morning!" Anancy said.

"Good morning, Anancy," all the women said, looking at him.

On his left, the woman looking up at him had the deepest and saddest hungry eyes he ever saw. "Take this corncob," he said, handing it to her.

The woman thanked Anancy. "You are on a journey?" she asked.

"Yes," he said.

She picked up a gourd of water and handed it to him. "Take this. You'll be hot and thirsty." He thanked the woman.

Anancy walked on, carrying the gourd of water. He came to a family digging their land, making earth mounds and planting yams in them.

Everyone sweated—the young man, the young woman, the mother, the father. Anancy gave the sweating family the gourd of water. The family gave Anancy a yam, happily.

Anancy walked on, carrying the yam. He came to a little open shed where a blacksmith was beating a piece of iron. As he worked the blacksmith ate charcoal with his sweat all over it.

"Why do you eat charcoal?" Anancy said. "Why? Why?"

"Have nothing else," the blacksmith said as he kept on working and eating the
sweaty charcoal.

Anancy held up the yam to the blacksmith. "Oh, please don't eat charcoal. Don't!
Take this yam. Take it, roast it, and eat it instead."

The blacksmith took the yam. He picked up a short-handled hoe and gave it to Anancy.

Anancy walked on, carrying the hoe. He came to a man who was struggling to break palm nuts open with a stone. Anancy gave the man the hoe to use. The man took a half bottle of palm oil from his bag and gave it to Anancy.

Anancy walked on, carrying the half bottle of palm oil.
He came to a woman with ten children around her in their
open yard. She was oiling her children's bodies with her spittle.
Anancy said, "Why do you oil your children with your spittle?"

"Have nothing else," she said.

"Oh, please don't use your spittle to oil the children," Anancy said. He gave the woman the half bottle of palm oil. "Use this instead."

The mother was grateful. She took the oil from Anancy. She thanked him. She said, "You take one of my children. Too many. Too many to feed. Too many. Too many to clothe. But first, *promise promise* you'll look after him well. *Promise promise* you'll bring him back *often often* to see his family."

"I promise," Anancy said. He took the little boy the mother offered. And Anancy walked on.

He walked on with the little boy. They came to a woman in a field, working alone. The lonely woman fed Anancy's little boy on a wooden spoon. And her head became full of new clothes he could wear. She put a string of beads around his neck. Anancy said, "Keep this child as company. But first, *promise promise* you'll look after him well. *Promise promise* you'll bring him back *often often* to see his family."

Happy, happy, the lonely woman said, "I promise! I promise!" And she gave Anancy
the wooden spoon.

Anancy walked on, carrying the wooden spoon. He came to a house where a woman was mixing corn flour in a bowl with her bare hands. Anancy gave the wooden spoon to the bare-hands corn-flour–mixing woman. The woman gave Anancy some corn flour.

Anancy walked on, carrying his little sack of corn flour. He came to a small herd of elephants drinking water at the pool of a stream. "Good afternoon, elephants!"

The elephants looked up. "Good afternoon, Anancy."

Anancy held up his little sack of corn flour. "If you elephants didn't have everything you wanted, I would give you this sack of corn flour."

There was a silence. Anancy was famous. The elephants were suspicious of him. They dreaded he might play a trick on them and get the better of them. He was famous for that. But an elephant said, "Well, Anancy, if you didn't have a small body, we'd lift this pool of water onto your shoulders and give it to you."

The leader elephant had thought out a way—a way they could be polite to Anancy and still control what happened. He said, "Anancy's good enough to offer us something. Let's offer him something."

"Yes. But—" an elephant said, "—what shall we offer him?"

"I'll tell you what," the leader elephant said. "Let's all jump over the stream together. And should anyone fall in, that one becomes Anancy's elephant."

Thoughtfully, all agreed. "All right. All right."

The elephants lined themselves up. And with a count of "One! Two! Three!" they jumped the stream, landing on the other side, except one—the youngest—who fell in. And that young one stood there, looking silly in the water.

In the midst of great elephant laughter, Anancy dropped the little sack of corn flour, walking all *pleased pleased* and proud to collect his elephant out of the water. Then, most unexpectedly, Anancy stopped, well taken up with something else. A little bird! The pretty little bird had been standing there all the time, watching all that happened. And Anancy was full of thinking, "Ah, pretty little bird! You will do very, very well for my little son, Tacoomah!" To catch the bird, Anancy began tiptoeing toward it, then he made a big leap and a grab, but missed.

The pretty little bird ran off over dry leaves on the ground, crossly saying, "Leave me alone! Leave me alone! Leave me!" It stopped. Its wings half dropped, its tail flicking up, it said "Churrrh! Churrrh! Churrrh!"

Tiptoeing again, Anancy kept saying, "Come to me, pretty little bird. Come to me! My Tacoomah will love you." He leaped at the bird with a grab and missed.

Once again the little bird ran off over dry leaves on the ground, crossly saying, "Leave me alone! Leave me alone! Leave me!" It stopped. Its wings half dropped, its tail flicking up, it said, "Churrrh! Churrrh! Churrrh!"

Anancy kept trying to catch the bird and missing. And the bird kept running away, crossly saying, "Leave me alone! Leave me alone! Leave me! Churrrh! Churrrh! Churrrh!"

Shocked, Anancy remembered his elephant in the stream. What! Forgotten my elephant? Anancy ran back.

He came back to the stream. He could not believe it. His elephant had run away.
Gone! All the elephants were gone. He stood, looking around and around. There
were no elephants. Not one elephant was anywhere. He remembered the corn flour.
Even that he didn't see. He gave up.

He walked away. Anancy walked on. He walked on, walking home. Empty handed!

So, you see it now. You see how the saying "don't leave an elephant to go and chase a bird" was started. He is the cause of it. He is the cause. Anancy!